RAINBOW magic

The Weather Fairies

To Alexandra 'Tink' Gunn
– a very special girl

Special thanks to
Sue Bentley

ORCHARD BOOKS
96 Leonard Street, London EC2A 4XD
Orchard Books Australia
32/45-51 Huntley Street, Alexandria, NSW 2015
A Paperback Original
First published in Great Britain in 2004
Rainbow Magic is a registered trademark of Working Partners Limited
Series created by Working Partners Limited, London W6 0QT
Text © Working Partners Limited 2004
Illustrations © Georgie Ripper 2004
The right of Georgie Ripper to be identified as the illustrator
of this work has been asserted by her in accordance
with the Copyright, Designs and Patents Act, 1988.
A CIP catalogue record for this book is available
from the British Library.
ISBN 1 84362 638 1
7 9 10 8 6
Printed in Great Britain

Hayley
the Rain Fairy

by Daisy Meadows

illustrated by Georgie Ripper

ORCHARD BOOKS

The
Fairyland
Palace

Forest of

Sweet Factory

The
Village
Hall

River

Wetherbury Village

Farm

Goblins green and goblins small,
I cast this spell to make you tall.
As high as the palace you shall grow.
My icy magic makes it so.

Then steal Doodle's magic feathers,
Used by the fairies to make all weathers.
Climate chaos I have planned
On Earth, and here, in Fairyland!

Contents

Water, Water Everywhere!

"I'm awake. You can stop ringing now," said Kirsty Tate sleepily. She reached out to turn off her alarm clock. That's strange, she thought, the alarm isn't ringing.

"Quack, quack, quack!" The noise that had woken her up came again.

9

Now that Kirsty was awake, she realised that it hadn't been her alarm clock at all. The sound was coming from outside. She jumped out of bed and peeped between the curtains. "Oh!" she cried. There was water right up to her windowsill, and a large brown duck was swimming past, followed by five fluffy ducklings! Kirsty watched with delight as the mother duck fussed around her babies, but then she frowned.

It had been raining really hard. In the front garden, the lawn and flowerbeds had disappeared underwater. Water lapped against the walls of the old barn, and beyond the garden gate the lane looked like a silvery mirror.

Kirsty rushed over to her best friend, Rachel Walker, who was asleep in the spare bed. Rachel was staying with Kirsty for a week of the summer holidays. "Wake up, Rachel! You have to see this!" Kirsty said, shaking her friend gently.

Rachel sat up and rubbed her eyes. "What's going on?"

"I think the river must have overflowed. The whole of Wetherbury village is flooded!" replied Kirsty.

"Really?" Rachel was wide awake now, and eagerly looking out of the window. "That's odd," she said, pointing. "The water isn't so deep in the garden and the lane. How can it be right up to your bedroom window at the same time?"

"Maybe it's fairy weather magic!" Kirsty gasped, her eyes shining.

"Of course!" Rachel agreed. She knew that fairy magic followed its own rules.

Kirsty and Rachel were special friends of the fairies. They had met on holiday with their parents on Rainspell Island, where they had helped the seven Rainbow Fairies get home to Fairyland, after Jack Frost's nasty spell had cast them out. Now Jack Frost was up to more mischief, and Rachel and Kirsty were on another secret fairy mission.

Rachel looked over at Doodle, the weather-vane on top of the barn.

Usually, with the help of the Weather Fairies, Doodle the fairy cockerel would be organising the weather in Fairyland. He had seven magic tail feathers and each one controlled a different type of weather. But Jack Frost had sent his goblins to steal the magic feathers, and they had run away with them to the human world. Doodle had given chase, but without his feathers, and outside of Fairyland, he had transformed into an ordinary metal weather-vane. Kirsty's dad had found him lying in the park, and brought him home. And that's where he would have to stay, until Kirsty and Rachel could return all seven of his tail feathers and send him back to Fairyland. They had already found six, so there was just one more left to find.

"Today's the last day of my holiday," Rachel said sadly.

"I know! We have to find the magic Rain Feather today," Kirsty called over her shoulder, as she quickly got dressed. "It's our last chance. At least with all this magical flooding, we can be sure the goblin who stole it isn't far away!"

As Rachel hurriedly threw on some clothes, there was a tapping noise at the window. "What if that's the goblin!" she whispered, nervously. The goblins were mean, and Jack Frost had cast a spell to make them bigger than usual.

There was a rule in Fairyland that nothing could be taller than the highest tower of the fairy palace, but the goblins still reached up to the girls' shoulders.

Kirsty put her finger to her lips. "Shh," she warned, edging towards the window. She peeped out, then threw back the curtains with a smile. An elegant white swan was tapping on the window with its beak. And a tiny fairy

was sitting on the swan's back, waving at the girls.

"Oh!" Rachel gasped in delight. "It's Hayley the Rain Fairy!"

Goblin Afloat

Kirsty was just about to open the
window and let Hayley in when she
hesitated. "All the deep water will rush
inside," she said.

Hayley laughed. It sounded like a
tinkling bell. "Don't worry," she called.
"It's fairy rain. It won't spill into
people's houses."

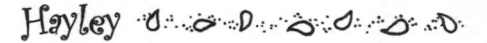

So, slowly, Kirsty opened the window. The water stayed where it was.

Rachel leaned forward and saw that a strange invisible barrier was holding it back. "It feels like jelly!" she said, poking her finger into it. The water beyond felt thin and wet, as normal. Hayley fluttered into the air and blew the swan a kiss. "Thanks for the ride!" she said. "Goodbye!" The swan dipped its head and glided away like a ship in full sail. "Hello, girls," Hayley sang happily.

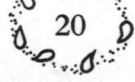

"Hello again, Hayley," Kirsty replied warmly. She and Rachel had met Hayley in Fairyland, along with all the other Weather Fairies at the beginning of their quest.

"We're so glad to see you," put in Rachel.

Hayley hovered in the air. She wore a pretty violet sarong-style skirt, and a matching top. Her long dark hair was tied up in a ponytail and decorated with a bright blue flower. She folded her arms and little droplets of blue and violet scattered from her silver wand. "Right!" she said firmly, her blue eyes flashing, "It's time that nasty goblin gave Doodle's Rain Feather back!"

"We think so too," Rachel agreed.

"But how can we go looking for him with all this flooding? We really need a boat."

That gave Kirsty an idea. "I helped Dad clear out the loft last week and we found an old dinghy. Let's go and ask if we can take it out to play."

Hayley dived off the curtain rail, her delicate wings flashing, and landed on Rachel's shoulder. She hid beneath Rachel's hair.

The girls found Mr and Mrs Tate in the kitchen. Mr Tate was looking baffled as he stared out of the window. "As I'm not going to be able to go in to work, I think I'll work on my mathematical theory about this flood water..." he murmured, wandering past them.

"Hello, girls," said Mrs Tate with a smile. "Your dad's trying to work out why the water isn't flooding into the house. But I'm just glad the place is dry! Toast's made. Help yourselves."

"Thanks, Mum." Kirsty picked up some toast. "Is it OK if we go out in the old dinghy?"

Mrs Tate smiled. "Sounds fine to me."

Kirsty and Rachel rushed out to the garage, munching toast as they went.

Kirsty soon found the dinghy and a foot pump and two wooden paddles. It didn't take long to inflate the dinghy, and then the girls put it out of the window onto the water. They climbed in carefully. It was just big enough for two people.

"Perfect!" said Hayley. She fluttered down to the front of the dinghy, where she sat like a tiny sparkling figurehead. Blue and violet droplets scattered from her wand.

"Here we go!" Rachel dipped her paddle into the water.

Kirsty began paddling too. At first, the dinghy spun in circles, but as they got the hang of steering it they began moving out towards the High Street.

Suddenly, a lady in a yellow mac and wellies leapt out in front of them.

"Look out, Kirsty! It's the lollipop lady!" called Rachel. She dragged her paddle in the water, using it as a brake. Quick as a flash, Hayley whooshed into Kirsty's pocket out of sight.

"People crossing!" said the lollipop lady, holding out her arms.

Kirsty and Rachel waited for a man to cross the road. He was pulling a floating, wooden box with a dog sitting in it.

"Thank you. All clear!" The lollipop

lady smiled at Rachel and Kirsty as they went on their way.

Outside the Post Office, they saw a group of village children splashing about happily. They all wore wellies and raincoats and didn't seem to mind the pouring rain at all. But not everyone was so happy about it. Kirsty spotted a cat that had sought refuge in an oak tree on the village green. "Poor thing," she said. "At least it's safe up there."

As they paddled past rows of cottages towards the park, Rachel saw a strange dark shape floating out from behind the children's slide. "Look over there. It's an upturned umbrella!" she said, pointing.

Kirsty's eyes widened. Four ducks, in a brightly-coloured harness, were quacking loudly as if they were very cross, and pulling an umbrella boat along. Inside sat a hunched, bedraggled figure.

Suddenly Rachel realised who it was. "It's the goblin," she gasped. "And he'll see us at any moment!"

Stop, Thief!

"Quick, hide!" Hayley shouted. "While we come up with a plan."

Kirsty and Rachel looked round desperately. The hut next to the bowling green was too far away and the goblin was approaching rapidly. There was nowhere to hide.

"What about the trees?" Kirsty suggested.

"If we become fairies, we can hide in the branches!"

Rachel was already taking out her magic locket, which the Fairy Queen had given her to use in times of danger. Kirsty found hers too and the girls sprinkled themselves with glittering fairy dust.

Kirsty felt her shoulders tingle as delicate fairy wings grew there. She fluttered straight into the air, heading for the nearest branch.

Rachel felt herself shrinking, but there was no time to enjoy the sensation of becoming fairy-sized.

She zoomed upwards on her gossamer wings and landed next to Kirsty. Quite by chance she spotted an empty bird's nest. "Quick! In here!" she whispered.

Kirsty and Hayley jumped in beside Rachel. The nest was lined with moss and downy feathers. It felt really cosy and dry. "Clever you, Rachel. This is a perfect place to hide!" Hayley whispered.

They weren't a moment too soon. The goblin in his umbrella boat floated beneath the tree. One of the ducks flapped its wings angrily, pulling at the stripy harness.

The umbrella wobbled and almost
tipped up.

"Oo-er! I nearly fell out then!" the
goblin complained, gruffly. "Stop trying
to get away, you stupid ducks. You've
got my lovely warm scarf for a harness.
It's me that's freezing! Atchoo!" His
loud sneeze echoed round the park like
a foghorn.

Kirsty, Rachel and Hayley kept as quiet as they could while they peeped out of the nest. They could see that the goblin was very thin, with enormous hands and feet. Rain poured from the brim of his battered sou'wester hat and dripped onto his long, crooked nose.

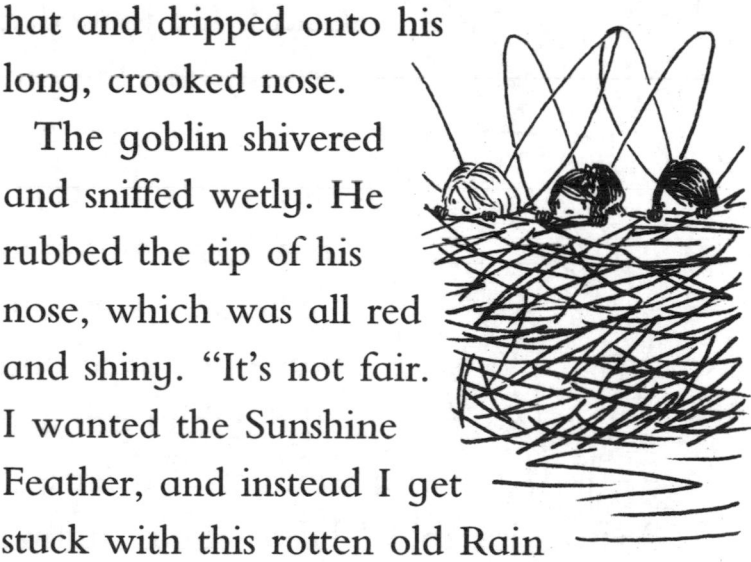

The goblin shivered and sniffed wetly. He rubbed the tip of his nose, which was all red and shiny. "It's not fair. I wanted the Sunshine Feather, and instead I get stuck with this rotten old Rain Feather! I should be toasty warm, not cold as yesterday's mud porridge and soggy as a squashed worm! Atchoo!"

"He's got a really nasty cold," murmured Hayley.

"Serves him right!" Kirsty replied.

Just then, the goblin lifted his hat and drew out a beautiful copper feather with silvery streaks. He jabbed it crossly into the air. "Stupid thing. Just stop this rain, right now!" he muttered irritably. The rain stopped at once and the goblin grinned with triumph. "At least it does as it's told," he grunted, stuffing the feather back under his hat.

"Oh, the poor Rain Feather!" whispered Hayley, indignantly.

Suddenly the goblin's miserable face
lit up in a grin. He had spotted the
girls' dinghy. "Oh, goody, a real boat
just for me!" he cried. Using his big
hands as paddles, the goblin steered
alongside the dinghy. Then he bunched
up his long legs, sprang straight up in
the air and landed, plonk, in the
dinghy. "Nice duckies. Let's harness
you to my new boat," he wheedled.
"That's it. All ready now. Off we go!
Mush! Mush!"

"Cheeky thing! He's stealing our dinghy!" Kirsty exclaimed. "And using the umbrella over his head."

"I feel like some more rain now!" shouted the goblin happily. He took out the Rain Feather and waved it in the air. A big grey cloud appeared above the trees and rain began to pour down. "Faster, ducks! Swim faster!" urged the goblin, his voice growing fainter as the dinghy sailed out of sight.

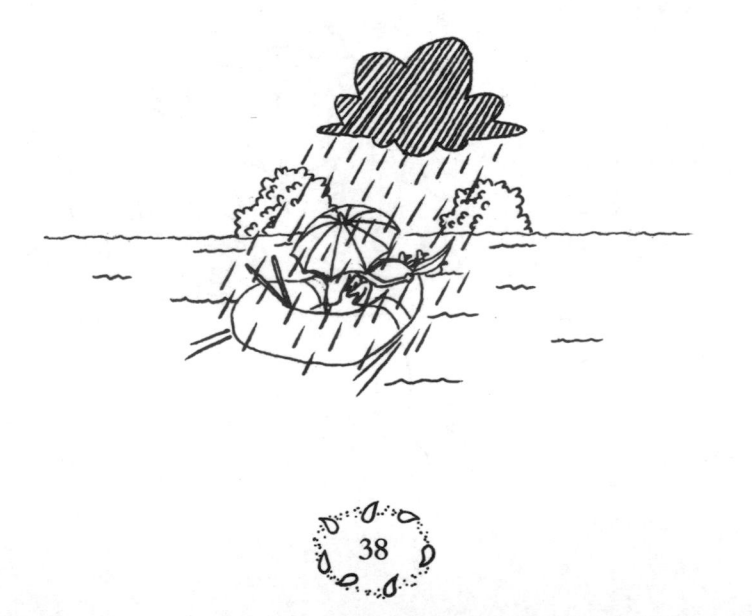

Rachel, Kirsty, and Hayley watched in dismay. "How are we going to get the Rain Feather back now?" Rachel wailed.

Feathered Friends

Kirsty stood up. "I've got a plan!" she announced.

"Hurrah! What is it?" Hayley asked.

"Remember how the goblin said he wanted the Sunshine Feather?" Kirsty began.

Hayley and Rachel nodded.

"Well, if we could find a feather that looks like the Sunshine Feather, then we might be able to trick the goblin into swapping!" explained Kirsty.

"It's a good plan. But where can we get a feather from?" Rachel said thoughtfully. "The magic feathers are really long and beautiful."

Kirsty grinned and flew into the air. "Follow me!"

Hayley and Rachel zoomed after Kirsty as she led them back over her house and towards the farmyard. The farmhouse and cowshed were centimetres deep in water.

Kirsty flew down and swooped through the henhouse door with Hayley and Rachel close behind. Inside, they saw fluffy dark shapes huddled on a perch above the waterlogged floor.

"Excuse me," Hayley said politely to the chickens. "We need your help."

The chickens looked up with dull eyes. "Eggs all wet. Feet cold and muddy. Feathers all soggy…" they squawked, sullenly.

"Oh, dear. They seem so sad," Hayley sighed.

"It's the wet. Dad says chickens really hate it. It depresses them," Kirsty explained.

Hayley flew down to stroke the chickens' heads. "Don't worry, chickens. We can make this rain stop with your help," she told them brightly.

"We need a big feather, as long as this..." Kirsty said, spreading out her hands to show what she meant.

"Why didn't you say so?" squawked a handsome cockerel. He twisted round and plucked a feather from his tail.

44

"Will this do?"

"Oh, yes. It's gorgeous. Thank you very much." Hayley fluttered down and took the feather. "Now, cheer up all of you," she said, flying towards the door. "We're going to go and stop the rain!"

"Thank you," called Kirsty and Rachel as they followed Hayley to the door.

The chickens fluffed themselves up, already looking much happier. They lifted their wings to wave after the girls. "Goodbye!" they clucked.

Outside, on the henhouse roof,
Hayley, Rachel and Kirsty looked
at the long coppery feather. "I don't
think the goblin will be fooled," Hayley
said doubtfully. "The Sunshine Feather
is flecked with golden yellow."

Kirsty grinned. "No problem. There's
a tin of yellow paint in our garage!"

They all rushed back to the garage.
Inside, Kirsty struggled to open the
paint tin. "The lid's stuck!" she
groaned.

Hayley tapped the tin with her wand, and a shower of sparkles twinkled around the lid, which promptly popped open. Moments later, Kirsty had painted yellow speckles on the feather.

"Perfect! It looks just like the Sunshine Feather!" exclaimed Hayley in delight.

"Now all we have to do is find the goblin," said Rachel.

Just then, a group of ducks flew overhead. Without a word, Hayley rose up in a cloud of violet sparkles. Rachel and Kirsty watched her, a tiny dart of light, as she flew alongside the ducks.

Soon she was back, and she had news for the girls. "The ducks have seen the goblin in the field behind the museum!" Hayley declared. "Come on!"

The girls followed Hayley to the back of the museum and, sure enough, there was the goblin floating across the flooded field in Kirsty's dinghy. "Atchoo!" he spluttered loudly. "I'm sick of being all wet and miserable. And my cold's getting worse."

Hayley, Kirsty and Rachel floated at a safe distance from the goblin. "Here goes," Hayley said, bravely. "I've got something you might like," she called to the goblin in a sing-song voice, waving the fake Sunshine Feather.

The goblin's eyes lit up greedily. "The sunshine feather! Give it here!" His long arm shot out and his fat fingers grabbed for the feather, but Hayley was quicker. She sped backwards out of his reach. "Oh, rats! Almost had two magic feathers!" said the goblin, scowling.

Hayley drifted forwards again. "I'll swap my feather for yours, if you like," she offered sweetly. Rachel and Kirsty held their breath. Would the goblin fall for their trick?

"OK," said the goblin. "Anything for some warmth. Now, give me it!" Hayley zoomed down and took the Rain Feather, thrusting the pretend Sunshine Feather at the goblin. He grabbed it and stroked it fondly with a wide grin on his face.

Hayley immediately waved the Rain Feather in a complicated pattern. "Rain,

stop!" she ordered.

The rain stopped at once, the grey clouds melted away and steam rose as the floodwater began to dry up. Then the sun came out, turning the shallow pools and puddles into molten gold.

The goblin waved his feather triumphantly. "My Sunshine Feather's working already!" he boasted. "I'm off now. It's about time I had a holiday." He leapt out of the dinghy and splashed away across the field.

Rachel, Kirsty, and Hayley hugged each other happily. "We did it!" Kirsty exclaimed.

"Yes, we've found all seven magic feathers!" sang out Rachel.

"Now we can return it to Doodle and
he can take charge of Fairyland's weather
again," said Hayley. She did a joyous
cartwheel in the air and violet and blue
sparks fizzed around her.

Kirsty was about to turn towards home,
when she suddenly shivered. "That's
strange. It's getting really cold," she said.

Rachel looked at her in alarm. "Oh,
no! Remember Doodle's warning? He said
'Beware! Jack Frost will come if his goblins
fail!'" There was a crackling noise as the
floodwater stopped draining away and
started to freeze.

Hayley paled. "It is Jack Frost," she
squealed. "He's coming!"

Frost Fright

A tall, bony figure, dressed all in white, suddenly appeared out of thin air. Icicles hung from his eyebrows and beard. "You again!" he snarled at Kirsty and Rachel. "How dare you meddle in my affairs?"

Rachel, Kirsty and Hayley gasped in fear as Jack Frost towered over them.

Kirsty looked at Hayley. "Go!" she whispered. "Take the Rain Feather to Doodle before Jack Frost gets his hands on it."

Hayley looked reluctant to leave, but she nodded and zoomed away, violet fairy dust streaming out behind her like a comet tail.

"As for you – you useless goblin!"
Jack Frost was saying. "I'll give you a
holiday you won't forget!" He lifted his
wand and sent a blast of
freezing white light
towards the goblin,
who was stomping
away across the
field. There was
a fizz and a
crackle and the
goblin became a
skinny, ice statue!

Jack Frost turned
back to face the girls
and gave a shriek of
rage when he saw that
Hayley had gone. He glowered at
Kirsty who was reaching for her locket.

"No you don't!" he snapped. He
pointed his wand and a narrow beam
of light shot out, freezing
both lockets tightly shut.
"Oh!" cried Rachel

and Kirsty. Without
their fairy dust,
they would have
to stay fairy-sized!
Jack Frost looked
down at the two tiny
girls. "What's the matter?
Cold frozen your tongues?" He asked,
and laughed nastily. It sounded like
footsteps crunching snail shells.

Kirsty trembled with fright, but she
looked straight into his cold, grey eyes.
"Why can't you live in peace with all
the other fairies?" she asked.

"Yes. Fairyland is a wonderful place. Everyone would be your friend if you stopped making mischief," Rachel added.

Jack Frost's mouth tightened with surprise. He seemed speechless. For a moment, Rachel and Kirsty wondered if he would listen to reason. Then Kirsty's heart sank as Jack Frost frowned.

"How dare you give me advice?" he roared, his eyes as cold as a glacier. "You two have interfered once too often, I think it's time I got rid of you for good!" He raised his wand.

Rachel grabbed Kirsty's arm and pulled
her behind a nearby tree, just as
a blast of freezing white light poured
out of the wand. There was a loud
snapping sound and thick white ice
coated the tree.

Kirsty and Rachel shivered with cold and fear. Jack Frost stepped round the tree and raised his wand again. Rachel heard a rushing sound and squeezed her eyes shut, expecting to feel an icy blast at any moment...

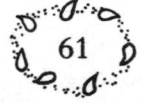

Rainbow's End

But, instead, Rachel heard Jack
Frost give a scream of rage, so she
opened her eyes.

Doodle, the fairy cockerel, was
approaching in a great rush of wind
and fire. His magnificent tail
glittered with sparks of red and gold
and copper. "Get away from them,

Jack Frost!" he ordered, his beak
snapping with rage. He flapped his
wings and a stream of white-hot
sparks sprayed from them and sizzled
on the ice.

"Ouch! Stop that!" cried Jack Frost,
backing away as several sparks landed
on his robe. Little puffs of steam
leaked from his spiky hair and beard.

"Doodle's come to save
us!" breathed Kirsty.
"And he's his true
fairy-self again!"

Hayley flew over to
the girls. "Are you all
right? How brave you
were to face Jack Frost
while you're only fairy-sized."

"We had to. Jack Frost froze
our magic lockets shut," Rachel told her.

Keeping one fierce amber eye on Jack,
Doodle came over and swept Rachel, Kirsty,
and Hayley under one wing. Then he
peered down his beak at Jack Frost. "You
must pay for what you've done!" he said
severely. "Not only have you brought havoc
to the weather, but you have threatened
two of Fairyland's dearest friends!"

Jack Frost cowered, melting ice ran
down his face and dripped
from his sharp nose.
"They shouldn't have
stuck their noses into
my business,"
he sulked.

"What if Jack
Frost casts
a spell on
Doodle?" Rachel
asked anxiously.

Hayley shook
her head. "Now he
has all his feathers
back, Doodle is seven
times as powerful as any
one fairy. He's more than
a match for Jack Frost!"

Doodle fluttered his magic tail
feathers. Coloured sparks shot
out and a rainbow began
rising from the ground.
Jack Frost started
spinning helplessly
round and round.
"Stop! Help!"
he cried. The
rainbow swept
him up, as it
shot into the sky
in a brilliant arc.
Jack Frost struggled
and yelled, but he
was soon a distant speck
amidst the glowing colours.
Kirsty and Rachel were still
staring after him, when they felt

themselves being whisked up in
a whirlwind of shimmering fairy dust.
With Hayley and Doodle, they sped
through a sky of cornflower
blue. Soft feathers floated
round them and they
could smell sweet,
summer flowers.
"Oh," breathed
Rachel with delight.
She caught a glimpse
of green fields and
red and white toadstool
houses. Then some clouds
parted and there were the
turrets of the fabulous fairy palace,
gleaming in the sunshine!

"It's Fairyland! And look, the
weather's still mixed up!" cried Kirsty.

A crowd of fairies waved and cheered
as Doodle and the girls stepped into
the courtyard of the fairy palace. King
Oberon and Queen Titania were
waiting to greet them.

"Welcome back, Doodle. We have
missed our weather cockerel," said
the King and Queen warmly. "And
our heartfelt thanks to you, Rachel
and Kirsty."

All the people of Fairyland cheered again and the Weather Fairies clustered happily around Doodle, eager to get back to their weather work.

"What's going to happen to Jack Frost, Your Majesties?" Kirsty asked.

Titania looked stern. "He can stay at the end of the rainbow until he sees the error of his ways. He's gone too far this time," she said.

Kirsty and Rachel smiled with relief. That should keep him out of mischief for a while, Rachel thought.

"We'd better give our magic lockets back," she said to Kirsty.

Oberon shook his head. "You must keep them, my dears." He waved his hand over the lockets. Silver sprinkles shot out of his fingers and tiny bells rang. "I have filled them with new fairy dust. If you ever need help yourselves, this dust will whisk you straight to Fairyland."

"Where you will always be welcome," added Titania, with a sweet smile.

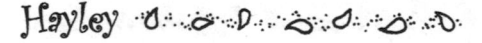

Kirsty and Rachel's eyes opened wide.
This was a great honour!

Then Doodle came forward. "I have
a gift for you, too," he said, and gave
them a weather-vane that
looked just like him.
"Oh! Thank you
all so much," said
the girls. They
hugged each of
the Weather
Fairies and said
goodbye to Doodle
and the Fairy King
and Queen. Then a
whirlwind of sparkling
fairy dust swept them
upwards and in a few moments they
landed back in Kirsty's garden.

Kirsty's dad appeared from behind the barn, looking puzzled. "Oh, you've found that old weather-vane. I've been looking for it everywhere. Where was it?"

"It appeared by magic," Kirsty told him, her eyes sparkling. Rachel smiled.

Mr Tate laughed, scratching his head. "Well, I'd better put it back. I've got used to seeing it up there."

"Me too," Kirsty agreed.

Just as Mr Tate was putting the
weather-vane up, a car turned
into the drive.

"It's Mum and Dad!" Rachel said,
waving.

"Hello, you two. Have you had a
good week?" asked Mr and Mrs
Walker, as they climbed out of the car.

"The best! It's been really magical!"
Rachel replied, hugging her parents.

The girls went upstairs to get
Rachel's things together,
while their parents had
tea in the kitchen.
Then it was time
for Rachel to
leave. Kirsty
hugged her
friend goodbye.

"You must
come and visit
us soon," Mrs
Walker said
to Kirsty.

"Yes, do!"
Rachel added.

"I'd love to, thanks,"
Kirsty smiled. "Goodbye, Rachel.
See you next holidays!"

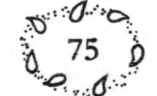

After Rachel had gone, Kirsty stood
in the garden thinking about all their
adventures. She looked up at the barn
roof. For a moment, a shining
rainbow touched the old tiles and
the weather-vane spun round swiftly.
As it did so, Kirsty could have sworn
she saw the cockerel wink at her
cheekily, and sparkle with fairy magic.

RUBY THE RED FAIRY
1-84362-016-2

AMBER THE ORANGE FAIRY
1-84362-017-0

SAFFRON THE YELLOW FAIRY
1-84362-018-9

FERN THE GREEN FAIRY
1-84362-019-7

SKY THE BLUE FAIRY
1-84362-020-0

IZZY THE INDIGO FAIRY
1-84362-021-9

HEATHER THE VIOLET FAIRY
1-84362-022-7

The Weather Fairies

CRYSTAL THE SNOW FAIRY
1-84362-633-0

ABIGAIL THE BREEZE FAIRY   1-84362-634-9

PEARL THE CLOUD FAIRY   1-84362-635-7

GOLDIE THE SUNSHINE FAIRY
1-84362-641-1

EVIE THE MIST FAIRY
1-84362-636-5

STORM THE LIGHTNING FAIRY
1-84362-637-3

HAYLEY THE RAIN FAIRY   1-84362-638-1

Collect all of the Rainbow Magic books!

RAINBOW magic

by Daisy Meadows

Win a Rainbow Magic Sparkly T-Shirt and Goody Bag!

In every book in the Rainbow Magic Weather series (books 8-14) there is a hidden picture of a magic feather with a secret letter in it. Find all seven letters and re-arrange them to make a special Fairyland word, then send it to us. Each month we will put the entries into a draw. The winner will receive a Rainbow Magic Sparkly T-shirt and Goody Bag!

Send your entry on a postcard to Rainbow Magic Competition, Orchard Books, 96 Leonard Street, London EC2A 4XD. Australian readers should write to 32/45-51 Huntley Street, Alexandria, NSW 2015. Don't forget to include your name and address.

Good luck!

All Rainbow Magic books are priced at £3.99. They are available from all good bookshops, or can be ordered direct from the publisher: Orchard Books, PO BOX 29, Douglas IM99 1BQ
Credit card orders please telephone 01624 836000
or fax 01624 837033 or visit our Internet site: www.wattspub.co.uk
or e-mail: bookshop@enterprise.net for details.

To order please quote title, author and ISBN
and your full name and address.
Cheques and postal orders should be made payable to 'Bookpost plc.'
Postage and packing is FREE within the UK
(overseas customers should add £1.00 per book).

Prices and availability are subject to change.